The
Fish
and the
Frog

PAGE PUBLISHING
Conneaut Lake, PA

First originally published by Page Publishing 2022

ISBN 978-1-6624-8302-8 (pbk)
ISBN 978-1-6624-8304-2 (digital)

Printed in the United States of America

The Fish and the Frog

Who Gets the Log

DARRYL BAKER

Fin and Ribbit were two very different animals from two very different parts of the pond. The time has come for them to leave their nests and find a home of their own.

Fin, always an energetic little fish and full of life, was eager to leave, but Ribbit was a timid frog who had always enjoyed the comfort of his mother's nest.

The two boys gave their parents hugs and kisses, said their goodbyes, and set off to find their homes.

"Goodbye. I love you," they said to their parents before leaving.

After a short search, Fin found a nice-looking brush of grass close to his parent's house and entered the home feeling lucky.

"HEY, THIS IS MY HOUSE," shouted Ernie the Eel.

"I'm sorry, mister," Fin said, apologizing.

As he continued on with his search, he found a big crevice in a rock.

"This is perfect," Fin said to himself.

Heading inside, Fin started to move things around how he liked it. Just as he began to settle in, he was suddenly startled by Grumpy the Gator.

"GET OUT BEFORE I MAKE YOU MY DINNER!" he screamed as he chased Fin away.

Barely escaping, Fin spotted a little hole he could hide in.

"It's not big enough for me to live in, but I'll stay here for the night."

Fin was frustrated from the long, hard day.

Meanwhile, Ribbit the Frog was not having any luck either on his search for a home. After traveling a long distance, he finally spotted something to accommodate his needs—a rock, the perfect size for a little frog.

"Amazing" he said. "It's half in and half out of the water. This is great!"

Feeling his trip was worth it, he headed inside with high hopes, only to notice eyes gleaming in the back shadows and hisses echoing in the emptiness.

"S-s-s-something S-s-s-smells good. Dinnertime," whispered Sydney the Snake.

Ribbit didn't give Sydney the chance before darting out into the open water and spotting a sunken boat. Immediately heading in that direction, he was again chased away by Barry the Bass. Ribbit was swimming so fast he was not paying attention to where he was going.

WHAM!

"Ouch," Ribbit said.

"Are you okay, little one?" said a relaxing voice.

"Uh, um, I guess so," said Ribbit, dazed from the crash. "Who-who are you?"

"I'm Torty the Turtle." He chuckled. "What's your hurry?"

"I'm trying to find a home, and I keep getting chased away, and I'm scared—"

"Whoa, whoa, slow down, little buddy," Torty said, interrupting Ribbit. "How 'bout I take you to a vacant hole little ones like yourself use as a resting area. I'll keep ya safe!" Torty proclaimed.

"Thank you," Ribbit said in a grateful whine.

Torty escorted Ribbit across the deepest, most-desolate parts of the pond, keeping him safe the whole time. Ribbit was grateful for his new friend.

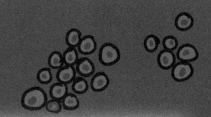

After a long and tiring trip, they finally reached the hole. Ribbit's little legs were tired, so he swam inside the hole and popped his head out to thank Torty, only to discover him fast asleep outside. Ribbit slipped away into a deep sleep with a smile, knowing his new friend was there to keep him safe.

The next morning, Fin awakened to see he's not alone.

"Hi," he said excitingly. "My name's Fin. What's yours?"

"I-I'm Ribbit," he stuttered in his usual timid manner.

"I'm looking for a home. What are you doing?" Fin said to Ribbit. Fin was a very energetic fish.

"I'm looking for a home too, and my new friend, Torty, is helping me," Ribbit said while pointing to Torty who was still asleep outside. The two were instantly friends.

Torty awoke to see the two playing tag. He was happy to see Ribbit had made another friend.

"Good morning, little ones," he called out "Torty!" Ribbit said loudly as he rushed over to him.

"Who's your new friend, Ribbit?" Torty asked.

"This is Fin, and he's looking for a new home too," Ribbit answered.

"Well, well. Welcome to the group," Torty said to Fin.

"Thank you, sir," Fin answered.

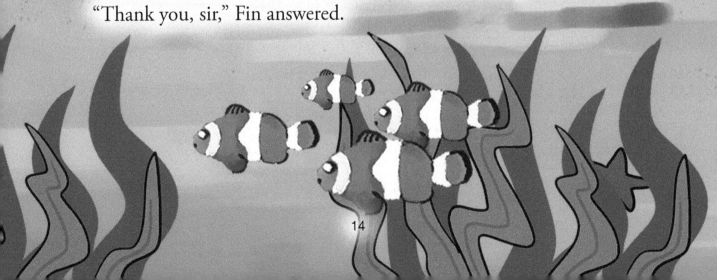

15

After eating breakfast, the three friends set off to find their homes. They looked at many houses but realized some were too big, and some were too small, some too deep, and some too tall. Fin and Ribbit started to lose hope. Noticing that his friends were sad, Torty encouraged them to take a nap.

Once they were sleeping, Torty headed to the surface, only to see a big storm heading their way. He quickly made his way back to Fin and Ribbit.

"Wake up, little ones," he said frantically. "We must make our way to safety. There's a storm coming."

Torty led them to a spot under a pier.

"This should be good for tonight," he reassured them.

When Torty woke up the next morning, he headed for the surface once again to check and see if everything was okay. Once he was satisfied, he woke up Fin and Ribbit, and they headed off. Not long after they left, Fin spotted a tree that had fallen into the water.

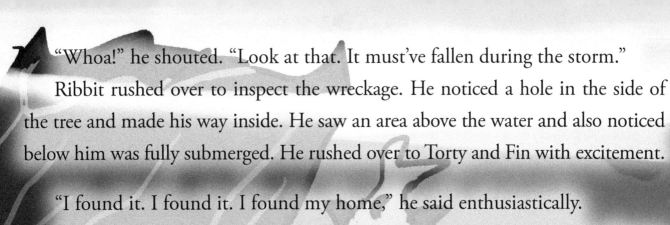

"Whoa!" he shouted. "Look at that. It must've fallen during the storm."

Ribbit rushed over to inspect the wreckage. He noticed a hole in the side of the tree and made his way inside. He saw an area above the water and also noticed below him was fully submerged. He rushed over to Torty and Fin with excitement.

"I found it. I found it. I found my home," he said enthusiastically.

He brought his friends over to show them. Fin quickly noticed it was the tree he pointed out.

"Hey," he said abruptly. "I found the tree first."

"Yeah, but I went in and seen it was empty," Ribbit answered back.

"It's not fair. You would have swam right passed it if it wasn't for me," Fin argued.

"And you would've never thought about living there if it wasn't for me," Ribbit said relentlessly.

"Little ones, please. Arguing solves nothing. It just causes more trouble," Torty said to the boys.

Fin and Ribbit swam away from each other in anger. After many failed attempts to bring the two together, Torty headed to the shore. He spotted a hare sitting by a broken tree stump. Torty noticed the hare was upset and went over there to see why.

"What's wrong, fuzzy one?" Torty asked the hare.

"You can call me Henry, Henry Hare. My tree fell into the pond during last night's storm, but it's okay. I'll just build another one."

Henry seemed to be okay despite the fact his new home just fell into the water. Henry explained to Torty that he shared the house with his best friend and that they would just work together to build a new one. This gave Torty an idea. He thanked Henry and hurried back to his disputing friends.

When he reached them, they were still arguing about who would get the house. Trying to talk over them, Torty finally screamed.

"Stop it now."

Because Torty was always so calm and patient, Fin and Ribbit immediately stopped.

"Instead of arguing who's going to get the house, why don't you two just work together and share it?" asked Torty while guiding them both inside.

"It is really big in here," Fin said to Ribbit.

"Yeah, we could both fit. I could take the top half because I like being outside of the water also, and you can have the bottom because you stay in water all the time," answered Ribbit.

"Awesome," they shouted together.

Torty was grateful his friends solved their problems and worked together. He decided he would make his home right next to them so they could always be together.

24

About the Author

Darryl is a devout father of four children to whom he dedicates his life to. He loves writing children's books that teach about morals and life's hardships while learning how to overcome them. He hopes his teachings of important life lessons help parents and children for many generations to come.

Lightning Source UK Ltd.
Milton Keynes UK
UKHW050609111122
411917UK00001B/1